THE
BEAR'S LUNCH

For Julius and Barbara

Puffin Books

Published by the Penguin Group
Penguin Books Australia Ltd
250 Camberwell Road,
Camberwell, Victoria 3124, Australia
Penguin Books Ltd,
80 Strand, London WC2R 0RL, England
Penguin Putnam Inc.
375 Hudson Street, New York, New York 10014, USA
Penguin Books, a division of Pearson Canada
10 Alcorn Avenue, Toronto, Ontario, Canada M4V 3B2
Penguin Books (N.Z.) Ltd
Cnr Rosedale and Airborne Roads, Albany, Auckland, New Zealand
Penguin Books (South Africa) (Pty) Ltd
24 Sturdee Avenue, Rosebank, Johannesburg 2196, South Africa
Penguin Books India (P) Ltd
11, Community Centre, Panchsheel Park, New Delhi 110 017, India

First published in Viking by Penguin Books Australia, 1997
This edition published, 1998
5 7 9 10 8 6

Designed by Deborah Brash/Brash Design Pty Ltd
Typeset in 24pt Sabon by Brash Design Pty Ltd
Made and printed through Everbest Printing Co. Ltd China

National Library of Australia
Cataloguing-in-Publication data:

Allen, Pamela.
The bear's lunch.

ISBN 0 14 056241 9.
I. Bears – Juvenile fiction. 1. Title.
A823.3

www.puffin.com.au

THE
BEAR'S LUNCH

Pamela Allen

PUFFIN BOOKS

Wendy and Oliver were going on a picnic.

When they spread out their
towels in the clearing,

they didn't know a big black bear
was out looking for his lunch.

First he looked under a log.
'AARRRGH…' growled the bear,

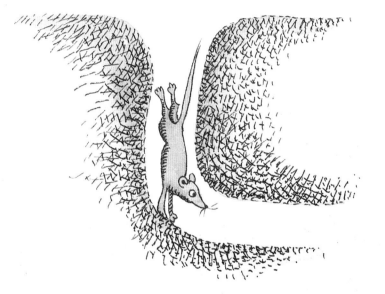

and a frightened mouse
ran into its hole.

Then he looked up a tree.
'AARRRGH…' growled the bear,

and a frightened bird
flew off into the sky.

He looked into a stream.
'AARRRGH…' growled the bear,

and the frightened fish
swam away to hide.

He looked behind some rocks.
'AARRRGH…' growled the bear,

and a frightened squirrel
scurried away as fast as it could.

Then he came into the clearing.
'AARRRGH...' growled the bear. 'AARRRGH...'

And the frightened children
ran to the end of the jetty.

The bear was hungry — by now *very* hungry.
He wanted his lunch. So he sat down on Oliver's
towel and gobbled up Oliver's honey sandwich.

Then he gobbled up Wendy's salad sandwich.
'AARRRGGH…' growled the bear.

Now the bear was thirsty.
'AAARRRGGH...' growled the bear.

He drank up all of Oliver's orange juice,
then he drank up all of Wendy's apple juice.

But the bear was a big bear, and that was
a little lunch. The bear wanted MORE!
'AAARRRGGH...' growled the bear as he
stood up, sniffed, and looked all around.

He could smell MORE at the end of the jetty.

'AAARRRRRGGH…' growled the bear.
He came closer.
'AARRGH… AARRGH…' growled the bear.
He came closer and closer.

When the bear was so close that Wendy
and Oliver could smell its hot breath,
and see its sharp teeth,
and look into its red rolling eyes,

Oliver let out an ENORMOUS…

'AAAAAARRRRRRRGGGGHHHHH!'
The bear took a step back.

'AAAARRRRGGGHH!' growled Oliver again.
The bear took another step back.

'AARRRGH! AARRRGH! AARRRGH!'
growled Wendy and Oliver together.
The bear was so frightened, he turned and
ran away as fast as he could.

Wendy and Oliver ran home to their mother.

When their mother heard about the bear she hugged them both tight, then made them another lunch. Wendy and Oliver were so hungry they gobbled it all up.

And the big black bear never came back again.